Pebble® Plus

Sharks

Hammerhead Shark

by Deborah Nuzzolo

Consulting Editor: Gail Saunders-Smith, PhD

Consultant: Jody Rake, member
Southwest Marine/Aquatic Educators' Association

Capstone press®

Mankato, Minnesota

Pebble Plus is published by Capstone Press,
151 Good Counsel Drive, P.O. Box 669, Mankato, Minnesota 56002.
www.capstonepress.com

1 2 3 4 5 6 13 12 11 10 09 08

Library of Congress Cataloging-in-Publication Data
Nuzzolo, Deborah.
    Hammerhead shark / by Deborah Nuzzolo.
    p. cm. — (Pebble plus. Sharks)
    Includes bibliographical references and index.
    Summary: "Simple text and photographs present hammerhead sharks, their body parts,
and their behavior" — Provided by publisher.
    ISBN-13: 978-1-4296-1728-4 (hardcover)
    ISBN-10: 1-4296-1728-4 (hardcover)
    1. Hammerhead sharks — Juvenile literature. I. Title. II. Series.
QL638.95.S7N89 2009
597.3'4 — dc222   2007051245

CKC
j 597.34

Editorial Credits
Megan Peterson, editor; Ted Williams, set designer; Kyle Grenz, book designer; Jo Miller, photo researcher

Photo Credits
Alamy/Danita Delimont, 19
BigStockPhoto.com/phred, 1
Bruce Coleman Inc./Ron & Valerie Taylor, cover
Dreamstime/Katseyephoto, 16–17
Getty Images Inc./Iconica/Jeff Rotman, 9; National Geographic/Brian Skerry, 20–21
Nature Picture Library/Doug Perrine, 10–11
Peter Arnold/BIOS Bios - Auteurs (droits geres) Cole Brandon, 15; Jeffery L. Rotman, 13; Jonathan Bird, 7
Shutterstock/Simone Conti, backgrounds
Tom Stack & Associates, Inc./Dave Fleetham, 4–5

Note to Parents and Teachers

The Sharks set supports national science standards related to the characteristics and behavior of animals. This book describes and illustrates hammerhead sharks. The images support early readers in understanding the text. The repetition of words and phrases helps early readers learn new words. This book also introduces early readers to subject-specific vocabulary words, which are defined in the Glossary section. Early readers may need assistance to read some words and to use the Table of Contents, Glossary, Read More, Internet Sites, and Index sections of the book.

Table of Contents

Hammer for a Head

Can you guess how
the hammerhead shark
got its name?
Its wide head looks like
the top of a hammer.

Hammerhead sharks live
in warm, shallow seas.
They swim alone
or in groups called schools.

A Hammerhead's Life

Hammerhead shark pups
are born live.
Between six and 42 pups
are born at one time.

Nine kinds of hammerheads
swim in the sea.
Bonnetheads are the smallest.
Great hammerheads
are the largest.

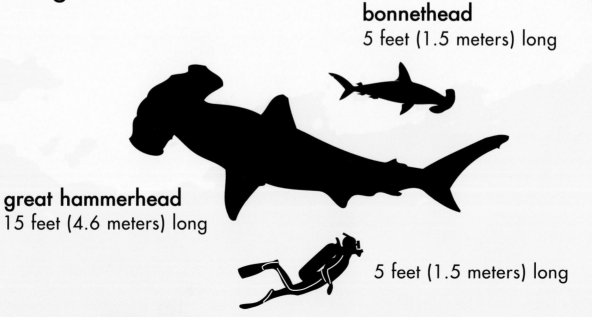

bonnethead
5 feet (1.5 meters) long

great hammerhead
15 feet (4.6 meters) long

5 feet (1.5 meters) long

bonnethead

What They Look Like

Hammerheads have an eye

on each side of their wide head.

They can spot prey easily.

Hammerhead sharks have
two dorsal fins on their back.
Dorsal fins help sharks
keep their balance
while swimming.

dorsal fins

15

Hunting

Hammerhead sharks hunt fish, stingrays, and other sharks. They eat crabs and squid too.

Hammerheads often hunt
on the ocean floor.
They look for stingrays
hidden in the sand.

Hammerhead sharks
can find prey anywhere.
It's not easy to hide
from these amazing hunters.

Glossary

balance — steadiness; sharks use their fins to stay balanced while swimming in the water.

fin — a body part that fish use to swim and steer in water

hunt — to chase and kill animals for food

prey — an animal hunted by another animal for food

pup — a young shark

school — a group of fish; as many as 100 hammerhead sharks might gather in a school.

Read More

Crossingham, John, and Bobbie Kalman. *The Life Cycle of a Shark.* The Life Cycle Series. New York: Crabtree, 2006.

Lindeen, Carol K. *Sharks.* Under the Sea. Mankato, Minn.: Capstone Press, 2005.

Thomson, Sarah L. *Amazing Sharks!* An I Can Read Book. New York: HarperCollins, 2005.

Internet Sites

FactHound offers a safe, fun way to find Internet sites related to this book. All of the sites on FactHound have been researched by our staff.

Here's how:

1. Visit *www.facthound.com*

2. Choose your grade level.

3. Type in this book ID **1429617284** for age-appropriate sites. You may also browse subjects by clicking on letters, or by clicking on pictures and words.

4. Click on the **Fetch It** button.

FactHound will fetch the best sites for you!

Index

Word Count: 146
Grade: 1
Early-Intervention Level: 18